MOUSE
LOVES SUMMER

by Lauren Thompson
illustrated by Buket Erdogan

Ready-to-Read

Simon Spotlight

New York   London   Toronto   Sydney   New Delhi

SIMON SPOTLIGHT

An imprint of Simon & Schuster Children's Publishing Division
1230 Avenue of the Americas, New York, New York 10020
This Simon Spotlight edition May 2018
Text copyright © 2004, 2018 by Lauren Thompson
Illustrations copyright © 2004 by Buket Erdogen
All rights reserved, including the right of reproduction in whole or in part in any form. SIMON SPOTLIGHT, READY-TO-READ, and colophon are registered trademarks of Simon & Schuster, Inc. For information about special discounts for bulk purchases, please contact Simon & Schuster Special Sales at 1-866-506-1949 or business@simonandschuster.com.
Manufactured in the United States of America 0418 LAK
Cataloging-in-Publication Data for this title is available from the Library of Congress.
10 9 8 7 6 5 4 3 2 1
ISBN 978-1-5344-2056-4 (pbk)
ISBN 978-1-5344-2057-1 (hc)
ISBN 978-1-5344-2058-8 (eBook)

The illustrations and portions of the text were previously published in 2004 in *Mouse's First Summer.*

One summer day . . .

Mouse and big sister
Minka come along to
play!

Where are they?

It is a picnic!

"Time to explore!"
says Minka.

Over here,
Mouse sees something
red and **juicy**.

What is it?

Drippy watermelon!

Under here,
Mouse finds something
black and **bold**.

What is it?

Munching ants!

Over there,
Mouse finds something
green and **tickly**.

What is it?

A grassy hill!

Up here,
Mouse spots something
blue and **bright**.

What is it?

The big, big sky!

Over here,
Mouse finds something
orange and **floaty**.

What is it?

A flying kite!

In here,
Mouse finds something
yellow and **tart**.

What is it?

Cool lemonade!

In here,
Mouse finds something
white and **crumbly**.

What is it?

Soft bread!

Mouse finds something **brown** and **smooth**.

What is it?

Yummy peanut butter!

Mouse find something **purple** and **jiggly**.

What is it?

Tasty jelly!

Minka takes a big bite.

Mmmm!

Mouse takes a little bite.
Mmmm!

Oh!
All around,
Mouse sees **tiny lights!**

What is it?

Glowing fireflies!

CRACKLE! POP! BOOM

What is THAT?

Fireworks fly,
every color in the sky!

Mouse and Minka
love summer!